Once Upon My Legs

Mike Dumbleton
and Sarah Boese

Once **upon** my blanket,

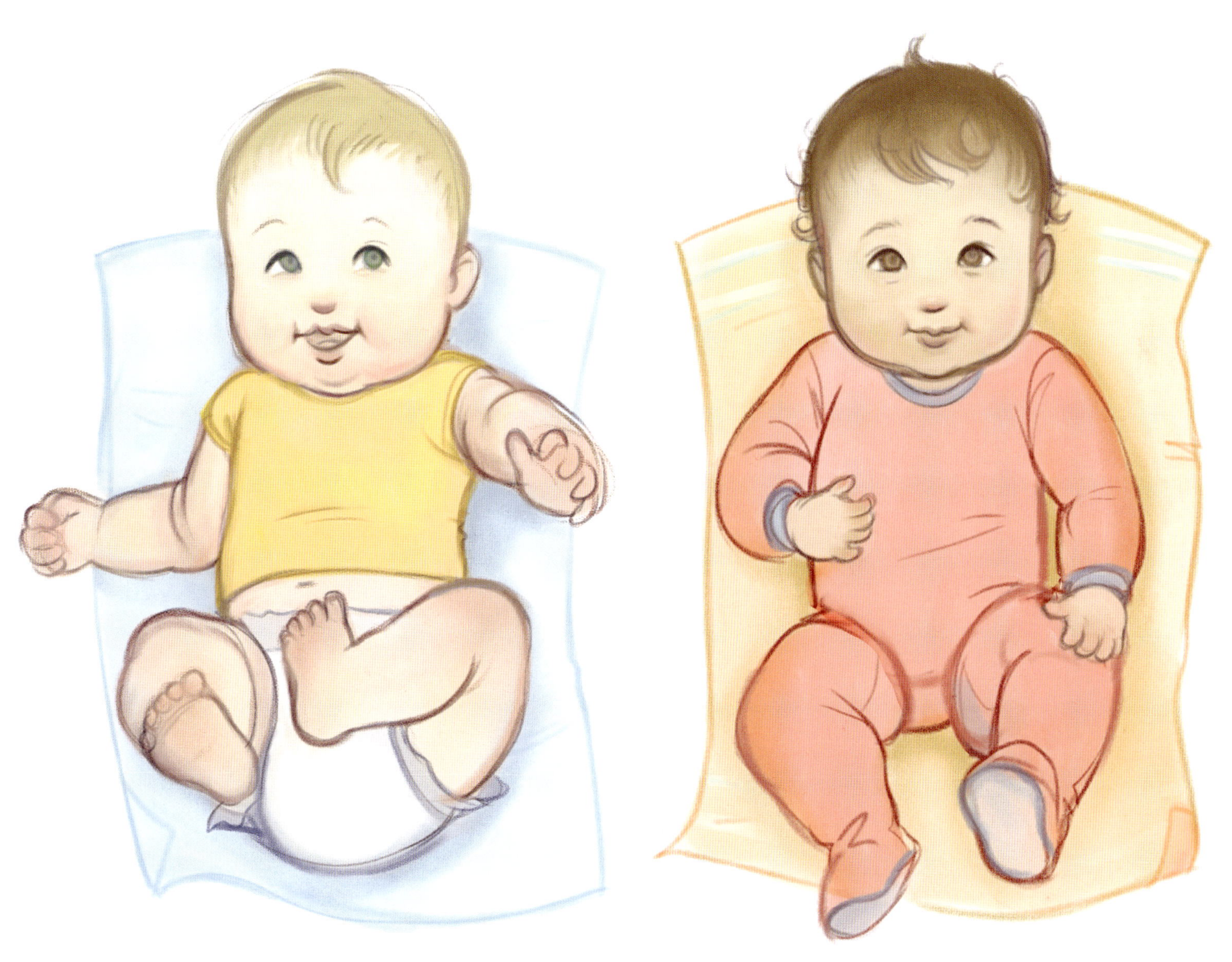

my legs **waved** in the air.

Bending,

wiggling,

waggling, not going anywhere.

Once upon my bottom,
my legs stayed on the floor.

Unless I **toppled** backwards,
then they...

waved around some more!

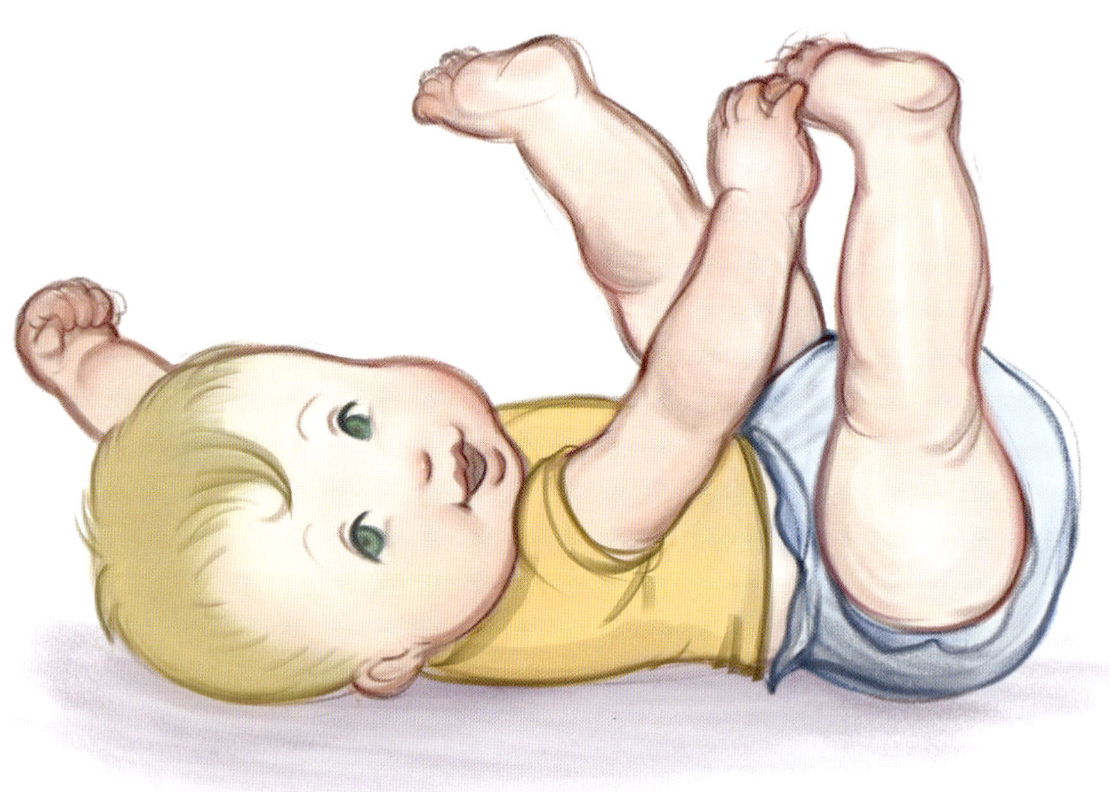

Once upon my tummy,
I could **move around.**

Slithering,

slipping,

sliding, all across the ground.

Once upon my knees,
my legs were often
sprawly.

But I could move much faster,
like a **creepy-crawly!**

Once upon my feet,
I really liked to stand,

by holding onto anything
that gave a helping hand.

The bookshelf,

the window sill...

the pot plant on the floor.

Clean clothes on the washing line.

The cat who lives next door!

Once upon my legs,
I started to **explore,**
every shelf...

and cupboard.

And every open door.

Mummy's
make-up,

sister's
crayons...

and **sparkly** stickers too!

Daddy's brand new sprinkler.
There's just so much to do!

I love it on my legs.

Life is **SOOO** much **FUN.**

Now stand clear
everybody,
just watch me...

climb and…

run!